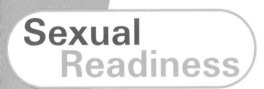

Sexual Readiness

When Is It Right?

by Julie K. Endersbe, MEd

Consultant:
Jennifer A. Oliphant, MPH
Research Fellow and Community Outreach Coordinator
National Teen Pregnancy Prevention Research Center
University of Minnesota

Perspectives on Healthy Sexuality

LifeMatters
an imprint of Capstone Press
Mankato, Minnesota

LifeMatters books are published by Capstone Press
818 North Willow Street • Mankato, Minnesota 56001
http://www.capstone-press.com

Printed in the United States of America

Library of Congress Cataloging-in-Publication Data
Endersbe, Julie.
     Sexual readiness: when is it right? / by Julie Endersbe
         p.   cm. — (Perspectives on healthy sexuality)
     Includes bibliographical references and index.
     Summary: Discusses various aspects of sex and sexuality, including
     physical risks, emotions involved, setting limits, and sexual
     responsibility.
     ISBN 0-7368-0274-6 (book). — ISBN 0-7368-0293-2 (series)
     1. Sex instruction for teenagers. [1. Sex instruction for
     youth.] I. Title. II. Series: Endersbe, Julie. Perspectives on
     healthy sexuality.
     HQ35.E53 2000
     613.9´07—dc21   99-29799
                                                 CIP

Staff Credits
Anne Heller, editor; Adam Lazar, designer; Heidi Schoof, photo researcher

Photo Credits
Cover: ©PhotoDisc/Barbara Penoyar
FPG International/©Ron Chapple, 28; ©Telegraph Colour Library, 42; ©Mark Harmel, 44; ©Steve Kahn, 47
©Index Stock Photography, Inc./10, 16, 17, 24, 48
International Stock/©Dusty Willison, 33
Photobank, Inc./©Don Romero, 22
©PhotoDisc/Barbara Penoyar, 26
Unicorn Stock Photos/©Richard West, 35; ©Jeff Greenberg, 38; ©Tom McCarthy, 53
Uniphoto Picture Agency/45; ©Terry Way, 18; ©Llewellyn, 55; ©Bob Daemmrich, 57; ©Lew Lause, 58
UP Magazine/©Tim Yoon, 6, 7
Visuals Unlimited/©Jeff Greenberg, 9

A 0 9 8 7 6 5 4 3 2 1

Table of Contents

Chapter Overview

Sex means being male or female. It means reproduction, or having children. Desire and intercourse also are part of sex.

Sexuality is how you understand yourself as a sexual being. It involves being comfortable with your body, your gender, your sexual orientation, and your sexual feelings and desires.

Sexual orientation is sexual attraction to or a preference for a certain gender—male or female.

Sexual development progresses in stages that begin at birth and continue into adulthood.

Chapter 1

Understanding Sex and Sexuality

Sex can be exciting, mysterious, and risky. Most people make a decision about when to have sex for the first time. Part of the decision is asking questions about the many parts of sex. There are also questions about the responsibilities and the risks involved with sex. This book describes issues teens need to consider when deciding whether they are ready to have a sexual relationship.

Sex, Sexuality, and Sexual Orientation

Sex is one part of sexuality. Sex means gender, or being male or female. It also means reproduction, or having children. When some people think of sex, they think only of intercourse. Penetration of the penis into the vagina, anus, or mouth is just part of sex. Sexuality, however, has many parts.

Human sexuality is complex. It involves how you understand and express yourself as a sexual being. It is the way your body develops and responds sexually. It is physical sexual behavior such as intercourse. It is also kissing and affectionate touching.

Sexuality includes how you feel about these sexual activities and responses. It includes your attitudes about sexuality—what you think is right and wrong or good and bad. It is being comfortable with your body, gender, sexual feelings and desires, and sexual orientation. Sexuality is a product of your individual life experiences that have shaped your feelings and values.

Sexual orientation is attraction to a certain gender. Opposite-sex attractions are called heterosexual. In a heterosexual relationship, a male and a female are attracted to each other. Same-sex attractions are called homosexual. Males who are attracted to other males are called gay. Females who are attracted to other females are called lesbian.

There are other kinds of sexual orientation. Some people are attracted to and have sex with both males and females. This is called bisexual attraction. Some people do not feel much attraction at all or do not have sex with others. This is called asexual orientation. Heterosexual, homosexual, bisexual, and asexual orientations are all normal.

A person's ideas and attitudes about sexuality constantly grow and change. Regardless of sexual orientation, each person must find healthy ways to express his or her sexual identity. If you understand the stages of sexual development, it may help you to understand your sexuality. It also may help you become ready for sexual activity.

I think you should talk with your parents about sex even though you might feel awkward at first. I never realized how much my mom knew about sex. She has struggled with sexuality all her life. I'm just beginning to understand my sexuality. But talking to my mom about my boyfriend helps me a lot. Parents can help.
—Miranda, age 17

Sexual Development

Sexual development progresses in stages. Each stage is part of a natural sexual progression. However, a person can experience more than one stage at a time. Sexual development does not suddenly begin when a child becomes an adolescent. Sexual development begins at birth and continues into adulthood.

Stage One: Sexual Exploration

Babies find their genitals, or sex organs, as soon as they control their arm movements. Between the ages of three and six, children become more interested in their own or others' penis or vagina. During play, some children safely explore each other's body while playing dress-up or doctor.

When children explore their own genitals, they masturbate. This is touching or rubbing the sex organs for pleasure. Masturbation is natural and normal. Starting early in life, people masturbate because it feels good. Masturbation is a private act that is a safe, healthy expression of sexuality.

Stage Two: Sexual Desire

Sexual desire often begins as an attraction to, or "crush" on, another person. For example, a child or teen may feel attraction to a famous musician, a teacher, or a friend. Often in such attractions the child or teen thinks about the other person a lot. It is a mental attraction. Both sexes have crushes. They may have a crush on a person of the opposite sex. Sometimes they have attractions to people of the same sex.

During puberty, sexual attraction develops into sexual desire. Puberty is the time when physical changes allow the body to reproduce, or have a baby. These changes in the body usually occur between ages 9 and 17. With these changes, a person begins to experience sexual desire. This desire is a physical attraction to someone—a desire to engage in sexual activity with that person.

Stage Three: Sexual Activity

Sexual activity happens when a person acts on the feelings of sexual desire. Sexual activity may range from only words and physical touch to sexual intercourse. This stage may begin during the middle school or high school years. The time is different, however, for each person.

The sexual activity stage may begin with flirting, gentle teasing, or holding hands. As this stage progresses, people may begin foreplay—arousing one another for sexual activity. Arousal can occur, however, without physical contact. Many things arouse a person sexually. For example, people can become aroused while watching a movie, taking a bath, or talking on the phone.

During foreplay, the body's physical senses are excited. This excitement sends sexual messages to the brain and genitals. Foreplay may involve holding, touching, or kissing each other. It can involve stroking or rubbing the genitals. Both the male and female body become very sensitive during arousal. Especially sensitive places are the lips, neck, nipples, inner thigh area, and genitals.

The body reacts physically to arousal. The penis, the male sex organ, becomes erect and long as blood flows into it. The penis also may begin to leak semen. This fluid carries sperm, which are the male sex cells.

During arousal, the female genitals become more sensitive as blood flow increases. The vagina becomes lubricated, or wet, with a substance called mucus. Lubrication of the vagina is the female body's way to prepare for the penetration of the penis. The clitoris, or female sex organ, becomes very sensitive as blood flow increases.

Most heterosexual teenagers begin having vaginal intercourse in their late teens, about eight years before they marry. The average age of first sexual intercourse is 17 for females and 16 for males.

When people are aroused, they may or may not have sexual intercourse. There are three kinds of intercourse—vaginal, anal, and oral. The penis penetrates the vagina during vaginal intercourse. During anal intercourse, the penis penetrates the anus. Oral intercourse is sucking or licking the penis, clitoris, or vagina.

Sexual intercourse is sometimes the end of sexual activity. However, it is not necessary for a person always to have intercourse after arousal.

Points to Consider

How are sex and sexuality different?

What is sexual orientation?

How does sexuality change when children reach puberty?

What is sexual intercourse?

Chapter Overview

A sexually transmitted disease and pregnancy are two risks of unprotected sexual intercourse.

Exchange of infected body fluids such as blood, semen, vaginal mucus, or saliva can spread sexually transmitted diseases. Protection such as male or female condoms or dental dams prevent the exchange of body fluids.

Pregnancy is a possibility any time semen enters or is near the vagina.

Being under the influence of alcohol or other drugs makes it difficult for a person to think clearly. This can result in not using protection, not respecting sexual limits, or uncontrolled anger leading to violence.

Chapter 2

Physical Risks and Problems Involved With Sex

Sex is a pleasurable and exciting part of life. However, when teens are deciding if they're ready for sexual activity, they should understand the risks and problems involved. Some risks and problems of sexual activity that affect the body are unprotected sex, disease, or pregnancy. Being able to communicate about such risks and problems is an equally important part of sexual readiness.

"To avoid STDs, never ever have sex without a condom or some other kind of protection. My friend Feliz got herpes. He never saw any sores or blisters on his girlfriend. He thought it was safe. Kids don't realize you can't see most types of STDs. That's why I'm waiting to have sex. I'm not ready to deal with the possibility of a disease or a baby yet."
—Gomez, age 16

Unprotected Sex

Unprotected sex means having sexual intercourse without barriers. Unprotected sex and having multiple sexual partners increase the risk for disease. Unprotected sex also increases the possibility of unplanned pregnancy.

Barriers provide protection during sexual intercourse. Barriers such as male or female condoms and dental dams prevent the exchange of body fluids. Disease is spread between sexual partners from infected body fluids. Body fluids that can be exchanged during sex are blood, semen, vaginal mucus, or saliva. Condoms and dental dams help to reduce the spread of sexually transmitted diseases (STDs). These barriers also reduce the possibility of pregnancy.

Sexually Transmitted Diseases

STDs can be spread through vaginal, anal, or oral intercourse. Each year three million teens acquire an STD. STDs are a physical risk for anyone who is sexually active.

Females are biologically more likely than males to get an STD. This is because of the way the female body is built. The germs that cause STDs have more places to linger and cause problems in the female body.

STDs can be very dangerous. They can affect a person's health for a lifetime. People often have no symptoms, or evidence of disease. Therefore, it can be difficult to tell if one or both partners are infected. Many times people don't realize they have an STD. As a result, they can spread STDs without knowing it. Some STDs cannot be cured. Other STDs, such as HIV, can result in death.

STDs don't just affect sexual partners. An STD can be passed during pregnancy from a mother to her child. Some STDs can be spread to a child through the mother's breast milk.

When a person has an STD, early detection and treatment are important to stop the spread of the disease. All STDs can be treated. Even with treatment, however, some STDs such as genital herpes never leave a person's body. Other STDs such as chlamydia can be cured if they are found early. Early treatment of STDs that can be cured prevents damage to the body.

A teen who is ready for sexual activity needs to understand STDs and be prepared to prevent their spread. Using condoms during sexual activity can be a healthy choice.

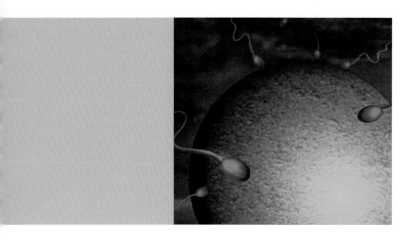

Pregnancy

Pregnancy is a possible result of sexual activity. A pregnancy can occur when the male ejaculates, or releases, semen from the penis into or near the vagina. Semen contains sperm, which may fertilize the female's egg. If the fertilized egg implants itself in the uterus, a pregnancy results. The unborn baby grows in this female organ until birth.

Each year about one million teens and their partners become pregnant. Among teens, 85 percent of pregnancies are unplanned. An unplanned pregnancy affects both partners, but it affects the female partner more. The female is pregnant for nine months and experiences many changes in her body. Few teen couples are ready to parent.

Pain During Sexual Intercourse

Pain during intercourse can be a physical problem involved with sex. Some females feel pain in and near the vagina during vaginal intercourse. This is especially common the first time a female has intercourse. This discomfort can happen when the penis first penetrates the vagina. It can result from too little vaginal lubrication, or moisture. Typically, this pain quickly decreases.

Pain during intercourse can be eliminated or reduced. Some
couples try a different position or slow down the sexual activity.
Water-based lubricants can help relieve vaginal dryness.
Lubricants help moisten the walls of the vagina, making it easier
for the penis to enter.

It is important for the female to communicate to her partner that
she has pain during intercourse. Together a couple can sometimes
solve the problem. If the pain doesn't go away or gets worse, the
female should see a doctor. Pain can be a sign of an infection.

Use of Alcohol and Other Drugs

The combination of alcohol and other drugs with sexual activity is
dangerous. Using alcohol and other drugs makes it difficult for a
person to think clearly. For example, a couple may not use
protection during sex. Also, setting and keeping sexual limits can
be hard when people are drinking or using drugs. A drunk or high
partner may not respect the other partner's sexual limits.

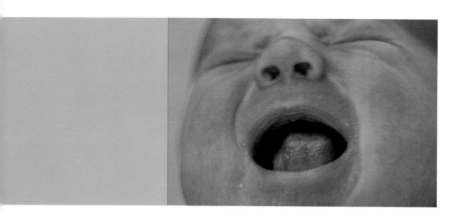

People who use alcohol or other drugs can physically harm not only themselves but also their unborn children. Drugs can harm the male's sperm and the female's egg. When that happens, a fetus, or unborn baby, may not develop properly. As a result, a baby may be born with problems such as fetal alcohol syndrome. This means that the child may have unusual features on the face. The child also may have trouble learning in school and throughout life. A woman who continues to use alcohol or drugs while pregnant puts the health of her fetus in danger.

Under the influence of alcohol and other drugs, some people lose control. Some people become angry or violent under the influence of drugs. Date rapes occur more often when one or both partners have been drinking.

A teen who is ready for sexual activity needs to understand the risks of sex while under the influence of alcohol or other drugs.

Points to Consider

Why is it important to use condoms during sexual intercourse?

Why is unplanned pregnancy a risk for teens?

What are two possible risks of being under the influence of alcohol or other drugs during sexual activity?

How can understanding the physical risks of sex help you to measure your sexual readiness?

Chapter Overview

Understanding and being able to identify your emotions helps you to determine if you're ready for a sexual relationship.

Being able to identify and express emotions constructively and appropriately increases the chances of having a healthy sexual relationship.

Love is a genuine feeling of care and concern for another person that usually lasts. Infatuation is a short-term attraction or desire for another person.

Chapter 3

Emotions Involved With Sex

A sexual relationship involves many emotions. Emotions and physical excitement combine to make sexual activity a wonderful experience. In fact, sexual intercourse is often called "making" love. Love is a strong feeling of affection for another person. People show love in many ways. One way that couples show their love for each other is through sexual intercourse.

Choosing to be part of any relationship can be an emotional risk. When sex is involved, the emotional risk can increase. This is because sex can change a relationship. Some couples may become emotionally closer through sex. The change in their relationship may be positive. Other couples may focus heavily on sexual activity. This focus can put the other parts of their relationship out of balance. Then the change may be negative.

The first time I was in love, I think I was ~Nikola, Age 17~ blinded by it. It was such a huge feeling.
Ben and I spent every minute together. It felt so amazing to be close to him, touching and kissing and all. Within two months after we started dating, Ben wanted to have sex. I loved Ben so much, but I hadn't thought much about having sex with him. I kept talking to him about it. I told him I wasn't ready to have sex yet. I'm still figuring out my feelings and what I want.

Dating

Teens who learn to understand and express their emotions are preparing for sexual readiness. Dating is one way teens can learn about themselves emotionally. It is a chance for teens to build a healthy relationship that is supportive and caring. Dating is one way that people decide what they want in a lifetime partner. It can help teens learn to deal with strong emotions and resolve conflicts.

Susan Neiburg Terkel has outlined some stages through which dating and relationships progress. Each stage may help a person to discover the joys and disappointments of a relationship. A relationship that generally follows these stages may be healthy.

Stage 1: Body Language—People signal with their body if they are interested in romance with someone.

Stage 2: Holding Eye Contact—Two people look directly at each other and hold eye contact for a few seconds longer than they normally do.

Stage 3: Small Talk—One person may begin a small conversation that attracts the other person or ends any interest in having a relationship.

Stage 4: Meaningful Talk—When a couple reaches this stage, they engage in discussion for hours. This is the stage in which a couple learns about themselves and each other emotionally.

Stage 5: Touching—Touching begins with a gesture such as a brush on the arm or holding hands. Sexual desire and activity increase as the relationship grows.

Identifying Emotions

Emotions are feelings such as joy, fear, or loneliness. If you can name your emotions, you may be able to understand why you behave in certain ways. For example, when some people feel excited and happy, they become outgoing and friendly. In contrast, when some people feel angry, they may become aggressive or even violent.

Once you can identify your emotions, you can understand them better. You can look to your past for clues. For example, anger is a common emotion that is neither good nor bad. A teen may feel angry because a friend broke a date. The anger may spill over into other relationships. When someone rejects you, you may feel lonely or angry.

To help you identify your feelings, the chart below lists some common feeling words. Learning what your emotions are may better prepare you for a sexual relationship.

Feeling Words

affectionate	sad	annoyed	bored
safe	jealous	scared	jumpy
left out	calm	brave	down
furious	confused	miserable	determined
embarrassed	excited	loving	empty
sympathetic	fortunate	foolish	fascinated
restrained	tense	overwhelmed	terrified
peaceful	helpless	threatened	guilty
pressured	trapped	relaxed	rejected
relieved	restless	ignored	happy

Expressing Emotions

Sometimes people have a hard time expressing their emotions. For example, some people think it is a sign of weakness to cry or to show affection. Other people may not recognize they are angry, so they explode at unexpected times. They have difficulty expressing anger constructively and appropriately.

Expressing emotions constructively and appropriately requires practice. You can learn to express your emotions through daily experiences. One way to practice is to use *I* statements. These statements help you focus on your emotions without placing blame. Look at this example of using *I* statements.

Kirby is 15, and his parents want him home by 10:00 on Friday nights. Kirby places blame if he says to his parents, "You are so unfair! All my friends get to stay out till midnight. You treat me like a child!"

Kirby expresses his emotions appropriately and constructively if he says to his parents, "I get the feeling you don't trust me when you set my curfew at 10:00. How can I earn your trust?"

Using *I* statements avoids placing blame on others and helps them to avoid reacting defensively. Conflicts arc more easily resolved and may happen less often when you use *I* statements. *I* statements are a positive way to share how you feel.

Healthy Emotional Outlets

In addition to expressing emotions appropriately, people need safe ways to deal with their emotions. It is important to recognize that all emotions are normal. However, the way emotions are expressed sometimes may not be normal.

Dealing with emotions, especially uncomfortable ones, can be difficult and exhausting. Usually it is easier to find outlets for pleasant emotions than it is for uncomfortable emotions. Even so, you can find some healthy outlets for uncomfortable emotions. Here are some examples of healthy ways to deal with different emotions.

These teens have learned some ways to deal with their emotions.

"When I get really frustrated, I head to my room and listen to music."—Maya, age 15

"Writing helps me work through my feelings. I can sort things out when I write in my journal."—Sam, age 14

"I used to break things or hit the wall when I got really mad. I've learned to go inside my head and think about how to calm myself down. I really try to avoid things that set me off."—Anna, age 17

"I've learned to meditate. The silence helps me to clear my head. It helps me erase my anxiety from the day." —Nou, age 16

"If I'm worked up, I run to burn off my stress. Exercise helps me deal with my emotions."—Joe, age 18

Joy—Try laughing, dancing, singing, or hugging someone.

Anger—Take time out to cool off before talking about your anger. Leave the situation. Exercise or work out to burn off anger. You will be able to discuss things more calmly after cooling off.

Sadness—Give yourself permission to cry or to grieve. Crying and grieving are very healthy ways to deal with sadness. Talk with a trusted adult or friend.

Jealousy—Avoid comparing yourself with others. Look at yourself in a mirror and say two things that you like about being you. Think of things you appreciate about yourself or about your strengths.

Sex and Emotions

Love is a strong emotion and is commonly confused with sexual desire. It is hard to know what being "in love" really is. You can love someone without sexual desire. For example, you may truly love your mother. This is love without sexual desire. On the other hand, you can have sexual desire for someone without loving the person. This is called infatuation.

True love exists when one person genuinely cares about another. True love usually lasts for a long time. Infatuation is an exciting, magnetic kind of feeling. It may be hard to think about anything else but one person. The feeling may be so strong that you are unable to see any of the person's faults. You can be infatuated for a short time with someone you don't know very well. Sometimes infatuation turns to love, but usually infatuation doesn't last long.

Sex with someone you are infatuated with may not have much meaning. Sex between two people who truly love each other can be a deep expression of their love.

Points to Consider

Name three emotions that you have felt today.

How does learning to identify emotions and finding healthy outlets for them prepare a person for a sexual relationship?

Your dating partner is jealous of the time you spend with friends. Write a response to your partner using an *I* statement that is appropriate, constructive, and nonblaming.

Why do you think it can be difficult to fccl or see the difference between infatuation and love?

Limits are boundaries, or points beyond which someone will not go. Safe exploration helps teens to set limits on their sexual behavior.

Standards are expectations of how a relationship should be. It is important to set standards for your relationships in order to have your expectations met.

Monogamy is a healthy standard in a sexual relationship. Two people are monogamous when they have a sexual relationship only with each other over a period of time.

Communication about sexual needs, possible outcomes of sex, and sexual limits is an important standard in a sexual relationship.

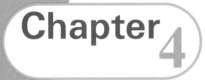

Chapter 4

Setting Sexual Limits and Standards

Limits are boundaries, or points beyond which someone will not go. Standards are expectations of how a relationship should be. Part of being ready for a sexual relationship is setting limits and standards for yourself.

Ninety-three percent of female teens report that their first sexual intercourse was voluntary. However, one-quarter of these young women say their first sexual intercourse was unwanted.

Setting Sexual Limits

Setting limits is an important part of sexual readiness. Relationships naturally progress toward more touching and physical intimacy, or closeness. Setting sexual limits for yourself can help with this natural progression. Each partner individually must choose the level of sexual involvement he or she wants. Additionally, partners must communicate to each other the level of involvement they want. Most partners at some point must decide whether to have sexual intercourse in their relationship.

Some safe exploration may help you to set your limits. Begin by thinking about what may happen in a sexual relationship. Think about what you are willing and not willing to do. Safe exploration may include asking your partner about things that you would really like to know. Ask yourself what you need to know from your partner that would help you to set your own limits.

Safe exploration also may include talking with a parent, trusted adult, or person older than yourself. That person's experience may help you think about things you might not have considered otherwise.

In setting your sexual limits, it may help to answer questions such as these:

Will I kiss someone using my tongue?

What parts of my partner's body am I willing to kiss?

Will I allow someone to touch my genitals?

Will I take off any of my clothes?

Am I willing to undress with the lights on in front of my partner? If not, am I ready for more intimate contact?

How will I talk about my sexual limits with my partner?

It is important to decide how far you are willing to go *before* any sexual activity takes place. Setting sexual limits is very difficult at the moment of sexual activity. This is because sexual desire and attraction can be intense. They can blur your judgment and decision making.

Over time, you may change your sexual limits. Just as before, these new limits should be decided outside of sexual activity.

Myth: "If you love me, you'll show it by having sex with me."

Fact: Many teens fall in love and decide not to have sexual intercourse. There are many other ways to show love. Respecting a person's sexual limits is one sign of love.

My girlfriend and I are committed to each other. Before having intercourse, we talked about our sexual standards. She told me what she expected from our relationship. It made me think about what I wanted from the relationship. Her ideas helped me say what I needed and wanted. I've been burned with past girlfriends. I wanted to be a part of a good relationship. It feels like I found one.

Toby, Age 19

Setting Sexual Standards for Yourself

Part of being ready for sex is deciding what you would like from a sexual relationship. Standards are the things you want or expect from a relationship from both yourself and your partner. They are needed in any sexual relationship. For example, you might expect public affection such as hand holding. Other expectations might be romance, a sense of humor, intimacy, and intercourse.

One healthy standard is to try to meet each partner's needs in a relationship. Sometimes one partner may want large amounts of time and attention. He or she may feel jealous of friends who get the other partner's social time and attention. On the other hand, the other partner needs more social time with friends. If both partners' needs are to be met, the couple must balance their time alone and with others.

Another healthy standard in a sexual relationship is monogamy. Two people are monogamous when they have a sexual relationship only with each other over a period of time. In a monogamous relationship, both partners are mutually committed to one another. Monogamy is a desirable sexual standard because it involves trust, respect, honesty, and commitment. Monogamy helps to reduce the risk of STDs. People who have sex with multiple partners increase their risk of STDs.

The chart lists other standards to consider in a sexual partner.

Does Your Sexual Partner Pass the Test?

Think about your answers to these questions.

Does your partner discuss sexual beliefs and limits with you?	Yes	No
Does your partner respect your sexual limits?	Yes	No
Does your partner keep your sexual life private?	Yes	No
Do you trust your partner?	Yes	No
Is your partner ever aggressive or hurtful during sex?	Yes	No
Does your partner pressure or threaten you to have sex?	Yes	No
Do you try to keep it a secret if your partner mistreats you?	Yes	No
Is your partner jealous of the time you spend with friends or others?	Yes	No

How did you do? For a healthy relationship, the first four answers should be yes and the last four answers no.

Once partners set their standards, they should not lower or ignore them. People don't always meet one another's standards. Those who accept less are sure to be disappointed.

Willingness to commit to a monogamous relationship may be one indication that you are sexually ready.

Communication

Communication is vital to any relationship. Couples who communicate talk about the good as well as the bad in their relationship. They share their emotions, concerns, and joys with one another. Through communication, they establish trust and honesty. They communicate their limits and standards to one another. Each partner should expect communication as a standard in the relationship.

For couples who choose to engage in sexual intercourse, communication is especially important. Communicating about possible outcomes before they happen is important. For example, couples should discuss how they will deal with a possible pregnancy before they have sexual intercourse. They should discuss the method they will use to prevent pregnancy until they plan to have a child. They should discuss what kind of protection they will use to prevent STDs. Protection is especially important if one or both partners has had other sexual relationships. This kind of discussion may help you decide if you want to have sexual intercourse with someone.

Couples need ongoing communication about their relationship—
sexual and otherwise. Talking about what is working and what
needs work helps relationships to grow. At its best, sexual activity
is a mutual experience. Both partners should gain from the
experience. If this does not happen, it is your responsibility to talk
about it or end the relationship.

Teens who are comfortable talking with their partner about sex
may be ready for a sexual relationship.

Points to Consider

Is it difficult to think about setting sexual limits during sexual activity? Why?

How do sexual standards help to build a healthy relationship?

Why is monogamy a healthy standard in a sexual relationship?

Why is communication important in any relationship?

Chapter Overview

A person who is sexually responsible shows respect for sexuality. He or she uses correct terms in reference to sex. He or she also does not abuse, exploit, or lie to get sex.

Using protection during sexual activity shows sexual responsibility. Such protection includes birth control methods, male or female condoms, and dental dams. Birth control methods only prevent pregnancy. Condoms help prevent both pregnancy and STDs.

People who care for themselves both physically and emotionally demonstrate responsibility.

Partners who take responsibility to discuss their needs and concerns improve the health of their relationship.

Chapter 5

Sexual Responsibility

Willingness to take responsibility is sign that a person is ready for a sexual relationship. Responsibility involves establishing, keeping, and respecting sexual limits and standards. It also involves showing respect for sexuality. It means having a plan to prevent unplanned pregnancy and STDs. It means taking care of yourself physically and emotionally. In a sexual relationship, partners take responsibility to communicate honestly and truthfully with one another.

Sometimes my friends sit around talking big about sex. They brag about the things they do and how they use their girlfriends and stuff. One day I just told them to be quiet. I said no girl would want to go out with them the way they act and talk. Girls and guys don't like to be treated that way.

Gil, Age 15

They were mad at first, pretending like they were all truthful and stuff. Now they don't act big and brag with each other any more. It was like I broke down some act. Now most of us can be honest with each other. One guy even asked for ideas about how he could treat his girlfriend better.

Respect for Sexuality

Showing respect for sexuality reflects a positive, healthy attitude. One way to show respect for sexuality is to use correct language in reference to sex and body parts. Using coarse or slang names for the genitals, body parts, and sexual acts cheapens sexuality.

Another way to show respect for sexuality is never to exploit or abuse another person. That means not lying to get sex and not taking advantage of others. Likewise, it means not allowing others to exploit or take advantage of you.

Sexual harassment is one form of disrespect for sexuality. Sexual harassment uses threats or power over people to force them into sexual behavior. Most companies and schools do not tolerate sexual harassment. Sexual abuse, rape, and sexual assault are the most extreme forms of disrespect for sexuality.

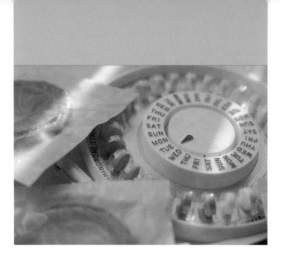

Preventing Pregnancy

Teens who are ready for a sexual relationship have a plan for using protection during sexual activity. Such a plan is an important part of sexual responsibility. This protection prevents unplanned pregnancy and STDs. A responsible action is to discuss and choose with your partner a method to prevent pregnancy and disease.

A health care worker can give advice on methods of birth control to prevent pregnancy. Three methods are birth control pills, "the shot," and implants. All three methods prevent a female's egg from being released each month. "The shot" is progestin, which is given to females through an injection. Progestin also is given as an implant under the skin. A health care worker must provide all three methods. All of these methods should be used with a condom to protect against STDs.

An emergency contraceptive pill (ECP) can prevent pregnancy if the female takes it within 72 hours after unprotected intercourse. The ECP is not meant to be an ongoing method of pregnancy prevention, however. Also, it won't work if the fertilized egg has already implanted itself in the wall of the uterus. A health care worker also must provide this pill.

Safer Sex

A major responsibility in being sexually active is to engage in safer sex. Safer sex means using condoms to prevent pregnancy or the spread of STDs. Condoms are an excellent choice to help prevent both pregnancy and many types of STDs. Most responsible sexually active teens choose to use condoms. Every sexual act should include latex (rubber) or polyurethane (plastic) condoms.

Intercourse is 10,000 times safer with condoms than without them. However, condoms do not protect against all STDs. A condom may not cover the entire area that an STD affects. Condoms only cover the penis or protect the walls of the vagina. STDs may affect areas other than these. Couples with an infected partner should talk with a health care provider. These professionals can provide additional information about measures to prevent the spread of STDs.

At a Glance

Condoms are effective when used consistently and correctly. It is important to know how to put on a condom before you need to use one.

1. Use a condom with every act of sexual intercourse, including vaginal, oral, or anal intercourse.

2. Store condoms in a cool place out of direct sunlight, not in wallets or glove compartments.

3. Check the expiration date on the condom package.

4. Carefully open the package to avoid ripping or tearing the condom.

5. Use a new condom every time you have sexual intercourse.

6. Use only water-based lubricants. Lubricants such as cooking oil, baby oil, hand lotions, or petroleum jelly can cause condoms to break.

7. Put on the male condom while the penis is erect and before sexual contact begins. Pinch the condom tip to remove any air. Slowly unroll the condom over the shaft of the penis, leaving a half-inch at the tip to collect semen.

8. While the penis is still erect, hold onto the base of the condom and withdraw the penis immediately after ejaculation. Then hold onto the rim of the condom and slowly withdraw the penis from the condom. Make sure no semen spills.

Both male and female condoms are available. Male condoms are made of latex or polyurethane. They cover the penis and collect semen during ejaculation. Male condoms are most effective when the female also uses a spermicide. This foam, cream, tablet, or gel destroys sperm. A female condom is a piece of polyurethane that fits inside the vagina to prevent sperm from entering. Condoms and spermicides are affordable and can be purchased in drugstores and other stores.

Dental dams are a way to protect against STDs for couples who have any kind of oral-vaginal contact. This prevents spreading an STD through open sores in the mouth or around the genitals.

Choosing not to have sex, or abstinence, is an effective method of preventing both pregnancy and STDs.

Sexual Readiness

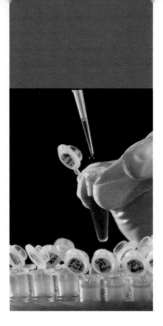

Physical Health Care

Teens show both responsibility and readiness for a sexual relationship when they take care of their body. That involves getting regular exercise, eating a balanced diet, and getting plenty of rest. It involves keeping the body clean by washing daily with soap and water. It also involves keeping the body free of alcohol and other drugs.

Physical health care includes regular checkups from a health care provider. These professionals can provide help in choosing a method to prevent pregnancy. They also can explain how to reduce risks to the body. Health care providers can perform regular tests for STDs. These tests not only show when a disease is present but also allow for early treatment. Such testing helps to reduce the spread of STDs.

Emotional Health Care

Emotional health care is an important part of sexual responsibility. Your emotions affect how you behave in relationships. Each individual is responsible for identifying and expressing emotions constructively and appropriately. You probably already know that can be difficult sometimes. Each individual, however, must take care of himself or herself emotionally in any relationship. It helps to find a partner who supports and values you. Even so, you're still responsible for your own emotional health.

Communicating With Your Partner

Taking responsibility to communicate with a partner is a critical part of any healthy relationship. That responsibility begins with each individual learning how to care for himself or herself. Partners need to identify their own needs and concerns. Then they must take responsibility to communicate their needs and concerns to each other. Ongoing communication helps to achieve a healthy relationship.

Points to Consider

Do you think it is difficult to use respectful sexual language? Why or why not?

Why do you think teens most often use condoms to prevent pregnancy and STDs?

One partner in a relationship is often silent and moody. When the other partner asks what's wrong, the reply is usually, "Nothing." Why is this kind of communication unhealthy?

What do you think is the most important sexual responsibility? Explain.

Chapter Overview

Readiness for a sexual relationship is a process that has several steps and happens over a period of time.

Teens may decide to gather more information before they are ready for a sexual relationship.

About half of all teens choose to abstain from sex during high school.

Some teens may choose to be in a sexual relationship without having intercourse.

Teens who are ready for sexual intercourse come to the decision thoughtfully. Their goal is to enjoy sex in a safe, healthy way.

Chapter 6

Your Future—
Making the Best Decision for You

Most teens are physically ready to have sexual intercourse at a young age. However, physical ability is only one part of being ready to have sex. Being ready for a sexual relationship in all other ways should be a thoughtful, multiple-step process. It is normal for this process to happen over a period of time rather than all at once.

I don't worry about being pressured into sex. I know exactly what I want and need in a relationship. My parents have been talking with me about sexuality since I was little. I don't think there is much that I own that is more valuable to me than my sexuality.

My advice is to believe in yourself. This helps me get along every day. Be proud of what you are. And what you can be.
—Tassie, age 18

One step in the process is understanding the physical outcomes and problems that may result from sexual activity. Another step, which takes time, is being emotionally ready to have sex. A third step is setting sexual limits and standards. A fourth step is understanding and being prepared to accept the responsibilities involved with sex.

Throughout the process of deciding whether you're ready for a sexual relationship, planning is key. The goal for sexual readiness should be to enjoy sexual activity in a safe, healthy way.

Influences on Sexuality

Many things influence a person's readiness for a sexual relationship. Parents, culture, peers, and community all influence a person's attitudes and beliefs about sexuality. Religious beliefs, maturity, and desire are other influences. How you view or value these influences may affect your personal readiness for sexual activity.

Another major influence on sexuality is the media. Some parts of the media are television, radio, magazines, newspapers, advertising, music videos, and Internet sites. You may have discussed the media in some of your classes. Therefore, you have learned how powerful its influence can be.

It's important to consider how these influences affect your decision to have a sexual relationship. You may want to consider whether you're doing what someone or something else influences you to do. Or are you doing what you want to do? Are you doing what you have carefully decided is right for you?

Am I Ready to Have a Sexual Relationship?

Consider the list of issues on the next page when deciding whether you're ready for a sexual relationship. Think about which statements you can check that apply to you. You might want to write down your answers on a separate sheet of paper. Your answers may help you decide whether you're ready for a sexual relationship.

Checklist for Sexual Readiness

- ◯ I am working on understanding my sexuality and on making it a positive part of my life.

- ◯ I understand that unprotected sex may result in a possible pregnancy or STDs.

- ◯ I am usually able to identify and express my emotions constructively and appropriately.

- ◯ I am able to set limits and standards for myself and keep them.

- ◯ I am able to respect others' limits and standards.

- ◯ I am learning to respect and enjoy my body.

- ◯ I can communicate with my partner about the possibility of pregnancy or STDs.

- ◯ I communicate my needs and concerns to my partner.

- ◯ I listen when my partner communicates his or her needs to me.

- ◯ I will buy and use protection during sexual activity.

- ◯ I care enough not to do anything hurtful to my partner or to myself.

- ◯ I have a respectful attitude toward my own and others' sexuality.

Even if you checked all the statements, you still may not be ready for a sexual relationship. You may need more information or choose to wait for the time being. You may be ready only to a point. Each person needs to make the decision individually in his or her own time.

Getting More Information

It is always useful to get more information about sexuality. Each person has resources at home, in school, or within the larger community. Talking or reading about sexuality and sexual readiness can create a greater understanding for you.

You could ask one or both of your parents to talk with you about how they dealt with sexuality while growing up. After all, they were the first ones to teach you about sexuality. They did this through their words, actions, and body language. Learning about your parents' experiences may help you to make your own decision. Also, this conversation might help to build your relationship with your parents.

Some parents aren't comfortable talking with their children about sex and sexuality. Then other people can provide information about sexuality. A caring, trusted adult can discuss concerns or fears about sexuality. Such people might be adult brothers or sisters, relatives, teachers, or friends. Some teens choose to talk with a counselor. Conversation with a counselor about these issues is strictly private.

In addition to talking with parents or adults, books are excellent sources of information about sexuality. Many adults and teens write and share their personal stories about sexuality. Reading what others have experienced can help you feel like you're not alone.

Choosing to Wait

Some teens choose to wait to have sexual intercourse. Around 50 percent of teens have not had sex by the age of 17. Although the percentage decreases as teens get older, some teens still choose not to have sexual intercourse. These teens choose to abstain from sex. Abstinence costs nothing, and it is an effective method of avoiding pregnancy and STDs. However, abstinence requires careful planning, such as setting and respecting boundaries and limits. It may take planning to avoid situations in which it would be hard to maintain your limits.

Abstaining from sex is a choice for now. You will have plenty of opportunity for a sexual relationship later.

Ready for Everything but Intercourse

Sexual desire and attraction are a natural part of growing up. Kissing and touching in a romantic way feels good. You may be ready for the kissing and touching. However, you may not be ready for sexual intercourse. If you don't choose to have sexual intercourse yet, your boundaries may look like this teen's:

I will talk with my partner about my limits.

I will tell my partner I don't want to take off any clothing.

I will tell my partner I do not want my penis (or clitoris) to be rubbed or touched.

I will enjoy this level of sexual activity and reevaluate my standards and limits later.

This teen has made decisions about sexual limits. The person has shared the limits with his or her partner. Setting sexual limits shows a person recognizes his or her sexual desire and wants to be responsible about sexual behavior.

Ready for the Responsibilities of a Sexual Relationship

Some teens feel ready for a sexual relationship. They understand the physical and emotional parts of a sexual relationship. They have set their healthy sexual limits and standards and communicated them to their partner. They are prepared to use protection before and during sexual activity to prevent an unplanned pregnancy and disease. They view sexuality with a positive, healthy attitude.

Points to Consider

Are all kids in high school having sexual intercourse? Why or why not?

What are two reasons a teen might choose to abstain from sexual intercourse?

Why is it important to wait if you're not sure you're ready for a sexual relationship?

Glossary

abstinence (AB-stuh-nenss)—choosing not to have sexual relations

boundary (BOUN-duh-ree)—a line that represents a separation of one area or limit from another

communication (kuh-MYOO-nuh-kay-shuhn)—the act of sharing information, ideas, or feelings with another person

emotion (i-MOH-shuhn)—a feeling such as happiness, love, anger, or grief

foreplay (FOR-play)—general sexual stimulation before intercourse; foreplay may include kissing, hugging, rubbing, caressing, or listening to music.

genitals (JEN-i-tulz)—sex organs; the male sex organs are the penis and testicles; the female sex organs are the clitoris and vagina.

heterosexual (HET-tur-oh-SEK-shoo-uhl)—attracted to individuals of the opposite sex; a male and female who are attracted to each other are heterosexual.

homosexual (HO-moh-SEK-shoo-uhl)—attracted to individuals of the same sex; males who are attracted to males are gay, and females who are attracted to females are lesbian.

intimacy (IN-tuh-muh-see)—closeness; people who share feelings with each other have emotional intimacy.

masturbation (MAH-stuhr-bay-shuhn)—rubbing or touching of the sex organs for pleasure

monogamy (muh-NOG-uh-mee)—an exclusive sexual relationship between only two people and no one else

pregnancy (PREG-nuhn-see)—a result of a male's sperm fertilizing a female's egg; a woman is pregnant when a fertilized egg implants in the lining of her uterus.

sexual intercourse (SEK-shoo-wuhl IN-tur-korss)—penetration of the penis into the vagina, anus, or mouth

sexual orientation (SEK-shoo-wuhl or-ee-uhn-TAY-shuhn)—sexual attraction to a certain gender (male or female)

sexually transmitted disease (SEK-shoo-wuhl-lee transs-MIT-ted duh-ZEEZ)—a disease that is spread through sexual contact between people

violence (VYE-uh-luhnss)—words or actions that hurt people or things that are important to them

For More Information

Bell, Ruth. *Changing Bodies, Changing Lives: A Book for Teens on Sex and Relationships.* New York: Times Books, 1998.

Bull, David. *Cool and Celibate? Sex and No Sex?* Boston: Element Books, 1998.

Endersbe, Julie K. *Healthy Sexuality: What Is It?* Mankato, MN: Capstone Press, 2000.

Harris, Robie H. *It's Perfectly Normal: A Book About Changing Bodies, Growing Up, Sex, and Sexual Health.* Cambridge, MA: Candlewick Press, 1994.

Theisen, Michael. *Sexuality: Challenges & Choices.* Winona, MN: St. Mary's Press, 1996.

Useful Addresses and Internet Sites

Centers for Disease Control and Prevention
1600 Clifton Road Northeast
Atlanta, GA 30333
1-800-311-3435 (CDC Public Inquiries)
www.cdc.gov

Planned Parenthood Federation of America
810 Seventh Avenue
New York, NY 10019
1-800-669-0156
www.plannedparenthood.org

Planned Parenthood Federation of Canada
1 Nicholas Street, Suite 430
Ottawa, ON K1N 7B7
CANADA
www.ppfc.ca

Sexuality Information and Education Council
of the United States (SIECUS)
130 West 42nd Street
New York, NY 10036-7802
www.siecus.org

Advocates for Youth
www.advocatesforyouth.org
Information for teens on preventing HIV, teen
pregnancy, and more

Kids Help Phone in Canada
kidshelp.sympatico.ca
Information, tips, links, and more that Canadian
youth can use in facing life's challenges

Sex, Etc.
www.sxetc.org
A teen-produced web site that deals with
health and sexuality issues

Sexuality Education Resource Centre
Manitoba, Inc.
www.serc.mb.ca/faqs.htm
Information on sexuality and sex-related issues

teenwire
www.teenwire.com
Sexuality and relationship information for teens

Index

Index continued

media, 53
monogamy, 35, 37
mucus, 10
multiple sexual partners, 14, 35
myths, 34

oral sex, 6, 11, 14, 46

parents, 8, 32, 52, 55–56
penis, 6, 10–11, 16–17, 45, 46
pregnancy, 13, 16, 18
    preventing, 37, 44–45, 47, 56
    STDs and, 15
    unplanned, 14, 16
progestin, 44
puberty, 9

rape, 43
    date, 18

sadness, 27
safer sex, 45
school, 43
semen, 10, 16
sex, definition of, 6
sexual abuse, 43
sexual activity, 9–11, 21, 23, 33
    deciding about, 51–58
    influences on, 52–53
    risks and, 13–19
sexual assault, 43

sexual desire, 9, 23, 28, 33, 57
sexual development, 8–11
sexual exploration, 8
sexual harassment, 43
sexual identity, 7
sexual intercourse, 6, 9, 11, 14, 21,
    32, 34, 37, 45
    painful, 16–17
sexuality, 6, 8, 52, 55
sexual limits, 17, 31, 32–33, 57
    and safe exploration, 32
sexually transmitted diseases (STDs),
    13, 14–15
    preventing, 37, 45, 56
    testing for, 47
sexual orientation, 6–7
sexual readiness, 53–58
sexual responsibility, 34, 41–49
sexual standards, 34–37
small talk, 23
spermicides, 46

Terkel, Susan Neiburg, 22
touching, affectionate, 6, 9, 10, 22,
    23, 32, 33, 57
transgender, 7

unprotected sex, 13, 14

vagina, 10–11, 16–17, 45, 46
vaginal sex, 6, 11, 14, 16–17